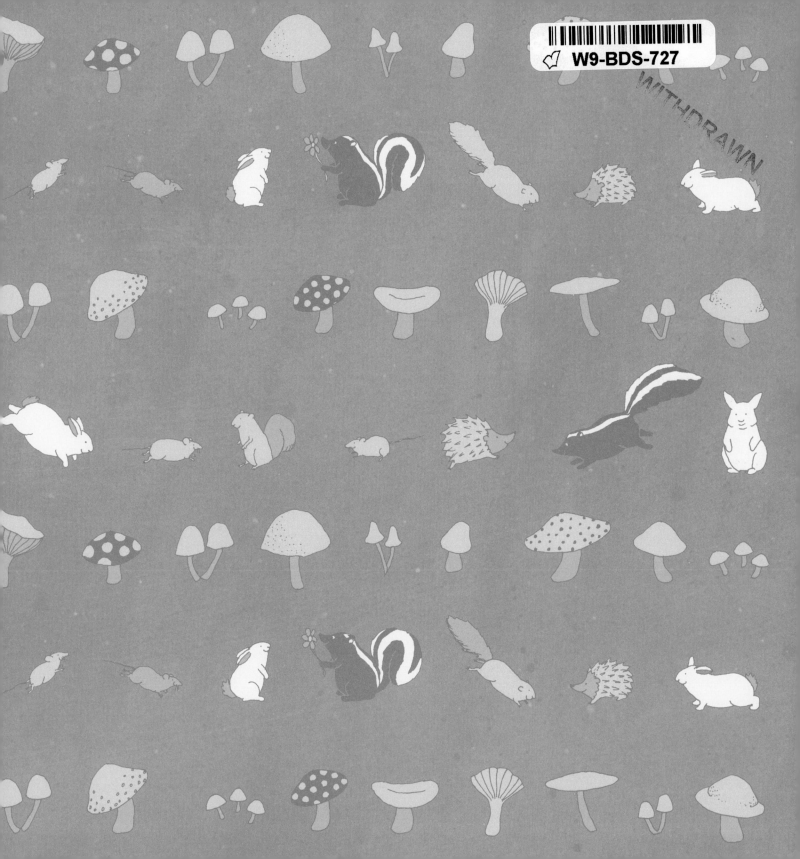

This Is the Glade Where Jack Lives

Or How a Unicorn Saved the Day

By Carey F. Armstrong-Ellis

Abrams Books for Young Readers • New York

This is the glade where Jack lives.

This is the tree that grows in the glade
where Jack lives.

This is the gnome that dwells in the tree
that grows in the glade where Jack lives.

This is the cake that fairies baked
that was brought to the gnome that dwells in the tree
that grows in the glade where Jack lives.

This is the imp, all warty and gray,
that steals the cake that fairies baked
that was brought to the gnome that dwells in the tree
that grows in the glade where Jack lives.

This is the mermaid, spritzing hair spray,
that trips up the imp, all warty and gray,
that stole the cake that fairies baked
that was brought to the gnome that dwells in the tree
that grows in the glade where Jack lives.

This is the faun, with pipe made of clay,
that jostles the mermaid,
spritzing hair spray,

that tripped up the imp, all warty and gray,
that stole the cake that fairies baked
that was brought to the gnome that dwells in the tree
that grows in the glade where Jack lives.

This is the troll, with thin hair astray,
that startles the faun, with pipe made of clay,

that jostled the mermaid, spritzing hair spray,
that tripped up the imp, all warty and gray,
that stole the cake that fairies baked
that was brought to the gnome that dwells in the tree
that grows in the glade where Jack lives.

These are the goblins who join the melee,
and rush at the troll, with thin hair astray,

that startled the faun, with pipe made of clay,
that jostled the mermaid, spritzing hair spray,
that tripped up the imp, all warty and gray,

that stole the cake that fairies baked
that was brought to the gnome that dwells in the tree
that grows in the glade where Jack lives.

This is the dragon, who's had a bad day,
and was roused from her nap and now enters the fray.

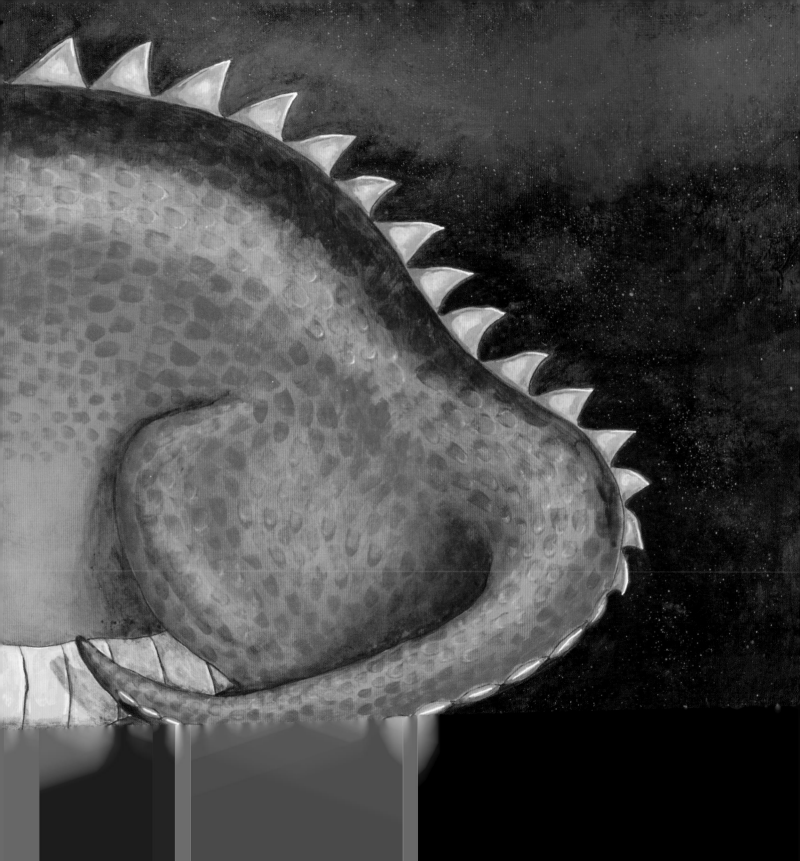

She swoops at the goblins who joined the melee
and rushed at the troll, with thin hair astray,
that startled the faun, with pipe made of clay,

that jostled the mermaid, spritzing hair spray,
that tripped up the imp, all warty and gray,
that stole the cake that fairies baked

that was brought to the gnome that dwells in the tree
that grows in the glade where Jack lives.

And this is Jack, all sparkly and bright,

whose magical horn shimmers
both day and night.

He kisses the dragon, who swoons with delight,

who kisses the goblins, who now feel contrite.

They hug the troll,
with thin hair astray,

who in turn hugs the faun,
with pipe made of clay.

He kisses the mermaid,
still spritzing hair spray,

and she hugs the imp, all warty and gray,

who brings back the cake that fairies baked

that was brought to the gnome
that lives in the tree
that grows in the glade where Jack lives.

**To Jane,
for her friendship and belief
that a unicorn can save the world**

The illustrations in this book were created using acrylic paint and ink.

Cataloging-in-Publication Data has been applied for and may be attained from the Library of Congress.

ISBN 978-1-4197-3850-0

Text and illustrations copyright © 2020 Carey F. Armstrong-Ellis
Edited by Howard W. Reeves
Book design by Steph Stilwell

Printed and bound in China
10 9 8 7 6 5 4 3 2 1

Abrams Books for Young Readers are available at special discounts when purchased in quantity for premiums
and promotions as well as fundraising or educational use. Special editions can also be created to specification.
For details, contact specialsales@abramsbooks.com or the address below.

Abrams® is a registered trademark of Harry N. Abrams, Inc.

ABRAMS The Art of Books
195 Broadway, New York, NY 10007
abramsbooks.com